Jenny in Space
by Andrew Willett

★

illustrated by Remy Simard

Scott Foresman

Editorial Offices: Glenview, Illinois • New York, New York
Sales Offices: Reading, Massachusetts • Duluth, Georgia
Glenview, Illinois • Carrollton, Texas • Menlo Park, California

When I woke up I could hear my mother calling me. It was a beautiful Saturday morning. Summer had just started. And it was just a week since I had passed my spacecraft driver's test. So, like any modern fourth grader, I wanted to spend my day zipping around the solar system with my friends. This was our first big chance to have fun in space. But my mother had other ideas.

"Jenny? Jenny, wake up! No time for sleeping! I need you to do some things for me today!"

I groaned and sat up in my bed. The warm breeze carried the smell of cut grass through my open window. Down in the yard I could see Bob, our robot, mowing the lawn.

My door opened. It was my mother. "Good morning, Jen! Did you sleep well?" She kissed my forehead.

"Uh-huh. Mom, do I have to do chores today? I wanted to call Ling and take a ride in Fluffy."

"You know, I still don't understand why anyone would call a spaceship Fluffy," said Mom. "Anyway, it happens that the things I need you to find for me are off-planet. So you can take Fluffy anyway." She handed me a list and a little money. "I need everything here by lunchtime. You'd better get moving."

I pulled on my glasses. Wow! There was some weird stuff on this list. I stumbled out of bed and found a clean spacesuit to wear. Then I called Ling.

"Gee, Jen," said Ling, "I wish I could go. But my mom has some stuff for me to do here. I can't. Sorry."

"Okay, well, I'm sorry too. Maybe I'll call you this afternoon, okay?"

"Um . . . sure, sure! We'll talk this afternoon."

Ling was acting kind of weird, but I didn't have time to wonder what was going on. I went downstairs.

"One bowl of Barbo Fazz cereal, please," I asked the food machine. While I ate, I looked at Mom's list again. It said:

- **ice (ten pounds, must be from a comet)**

- **salt (four pounds, from the salt mines of Orion)**

- **cream (three buckets, from the Havartian Space Cows)**

- **sugar (one pound, from the Great Rock Candy Nebula)**

- **snoob fruit (one basketful, from the swamps of the planet Marshmoop)**

The more I thought about this list, the less upset I was that I had to run errands for my mother. I was going to go to some exciting places! This could be an incredible adventure.

After breakfast I went out to the landing pad.
There was Fluffy, the best spacecraft anybody ever
had. She had a cool paint job, and she had all kinds
of special features. And she was pretty smart. Best of
all, she was much nicer than most spacecrafts.

"Good morning, Fluffy," I called. "Get ready
for takeoff."

"Good morning, Jen," Fluffy's voice came through
a speaker near the driver's dome. "I'm ready when
you are."

"Let's run some errands!" I shouted. Up we went
and out into space.

The first thing on the list was ice from a comet. "Fluffy," I asked, "are there any comets anywhere nearby right now?"

Fluffy paused for a minute. "Not anywhere too nearby," she answered. "Let me send out some probes. That will give me a better look around."

A bunch of bright green lights swirled out from under the ship. They dashed off in all directions.

"Stand by," said Fluffy. "Searching . . . aha! Plenty of comets over this way." Comets appeared on the star chart in front of me.

"Well, that wasn't so hard," I said. "Head for those comets!"

Soon we were cruising along next to a comet. It streaked through space, shedding slush and rock like a huge, dirty snowball. "Yuck! Comets are so grimy! We'll never get any clean ice out of this."

"Stand by," said Fluffy. "I'm scanning the comet. There's a big chunk of ice not far inside it. It looks pretty clean."

"Can you get it with your grabbing arm, Fluffy?"

"No problem," Fluffy replied. A shiny arm reached out from the ship and plunged into the comet. Soon it held up a huge chunk of blue ice. "What's next?"

"Salt. Plot a course for the Orion salt mines." And off we went.

From the air, the Orion salt mines looked like ant nests. There were robots everywhere, hard at work. Some brought out cartloads of dirt and rock from deep underground. Other robots picked out the biggest chunks of salt from this dirt. Still others moved all the leftovers onto a huge pile.

"Fluffy, look at those piles! The robots are leaving the littlest pieces of salt behind!"

"You're right!" said Fluffy. "The robots must not care about the little pieces. They only want the big ones."

"Fluffy, will you talk to the robots?"

"Sure. What shall I say?"

"Ask them if we can pick through the little pieces of salt."

Soon we had found plenty of salt. We put it into Fluffy's storage space, right next to the ice.

9

The planet Havarti is home to some very famous cows. This incredible herd lives in space. They float around and around the planet.

The Havartians have built dairy barns in space to milk these cows. They're space stations! Every time a cow goes past one of these stations, the Havartians milk it.

I docked Fluffy at a Havartian dairy shop and went inside. A salesman in a straw hat walked up to me.

"May I help you?"

"I need three buckets of cream, please." I handed him the money my mother had given me.

"Certainly. Let us put them in your spacecraft."

A robot rolled away with the buckets. I stood inside the station for a while, watching the cows float past. What a beautiful sight!

The Great Rock Candy Nebula is like nothing else in the galaxy. A nebula is a cloud of glowing gas and dust. This nebula is a cloud of glowing gas, dust, *and* sugar crystals. Some of the crystals are as big as your head.

Fluffy and I flew a little way into the nebula. Soon we couldn't see anything. It was like being in a room full of glowing fog. We stopped.

"Fluffy, send out some probes. See if there are any big sugar crystals anywhere." The green lights of Fluffy's probes vanished into the haze.

"I found one!" said Fluffy. "It's right next to us. Here, look!"

Fluffy's grabber arm appeared in the window. It held a huge crystal. The sparkling facets of the crystal glowed in the light.

"Wow! It's beautiful! Mom will love it!"

"Jen, do you know why your mother wants all this stuff?" asked Fluffy. "I can't figure it out."

"Who knows," I said. "Whatever it is, it won't be as much fun as this trip. What an adventure! And now there's only one stop left. Let's go to the planet Marshmoop."

When we got to the swamp-covered planet of Marshmoop, Fluffy had some bad news. "I won't be able to help you much here, Jen," she said. "Snoob fruit grows on the ground, beneath the trees. You'll have to look for them on foot."

Fluffy landed on a patch of muddy soil. I grabbed my fruit basket and hopped out. Suddenly there was an awful squishing noise. She was sinking into the mud!

"Fluffy, you're too heavy!" I yelled. "This swamp ground is too soft to hold you up! Take off!"

Fluffy rose into the air.

"Okay," she said. "Here's my plan. When you find the fruit, whistle for me. I'll come get you."

I set off into the swamp.

I was very glad I was wearing boots. The water sloshed at my feet. The mud made bubbly squishing noises as I stepped through it. Before long I found a patch of snoob bushes. My mother loves the bright purple fruit, so round and sweet-smelling. A jubjub bird looked at me and ruffled its dark feathers.

I picked snoob fruit as fast as I could. Soon I had filled my basket. I whistled loudly.

A silvery grabber arm snaked down through the tree branches.

"Jen?" Fluffy's voice came from above. "Take my arm and I'll pull you up."

As I rose toward my spaceship, I threw a piece of fruit to the bird. It caught the fruit in its sharp beak and swallowed it whole. Then it seemed to smile.

"That's everything, Fluffy," I said. "Let's go home and see what all this is for."

15

Before long, I was flying above my house.

"Look, Jenny," said Fluffy. "Ling is here with her family."

Fluffy was right. Ling's family and mine were in the backyard, putting food on the picnic table.

My mother met us at the landing pad. "Surprise!" she said. "We're having a party to celebrate your new spacecraft driver's license."

"So, what are you going to do with all the things I got?" I said.

"That's the best part. We're making ice cream! You use the ice and salt to freeze the cream, sugar, and fruit. I haven't had this since I was your age. Trust me, you'll love it. Just wait."

Mom was right. It was the best food I'd ever tasted. What an incredible day!